Let's Connect!

Thank you for taking time to read this story! I pray you enjoy it and that you will continue to follow my work as a self-published author who desires to change the world through writing! Please leave a review on Amazon at the link below, they mean everything and is always appreciated!

God Bless,
Author Aundrya Schnel

www.amazon.com/author/aundryaschnel
www.amazon.com/author/aundryatheauthor

Podcast - Ready Writers Ignite
Podcast - Mind Without Walls
Podcast - Aundrya Speaks

Who Wants To Write A Book?

I offer a master class where I teach men and women around the world of all ages how to write their first or next book along with the path to take for having their book published! If you have a desire to write a book, this class is for YOU! For more information and to register for the next class, please visit the website below! Thank you in advance for your support and I look forward to working with you in the near future!

God Bless,
Aundrya

writeyourwayacademy.square.site
writeyourway@outlook.com

TRIBUTE

My Late Mother

Minister Linda Darlene Collins-Richardson
July 4, 1959 – June 19, 2005

My Late Grandmother

Mother Harriett Richardson
October 10, 1931 – February 4, 2017

INTRODUCTION

"What did he say?"
"If I don't agree to the abortion, he's going to stop paying my mom's bills and take my scholarship for college..."
"See, girl! I told you! Daddy is not paying for us, college and a baby! Did you forget the agreement?"
"No, but I don't believe in abortion!"
"Well, you better believe in it today because if you keep this kid, you can say goodbye to college and say hello to the door he and the rest of the church throws you out of when he tells them you got pregnant by some random guy!"
"But I didn't get pregnant by a random guy, I got pregnant by our pastor!"
"He knows that but he's not taking the fall for you. The organization will kick him out and that's no money for any of us!"
"I just don't know..."
"Listen Nikki, I love you like a sister. We've been through a lot together, but I will not let you mess this up for me and the other girls who have literally bent over backwards these last four plus years to get this college money. We're going to graduate, take this money and get the hell out of here! Don't you want to leave?"
"Yeah, I do..."
"Then act like it! Speaking of sisters, did you forget about your younger sisters? They're on the limb for this money too! You don't want them to miss out do you?"
"No..."

"Okay, so why are we having this conversation right now? Look, I had my abortion last week and it was fine. You will be okay and you will be glad you did it!"
"No I won't. I won't be proud of killing my child. Look, I just can't do this! I don't want an abortion!"
"Nikki, do I need to remind you about the last girl who said they weren't going to have an abortion when Daddy got them pregnant?"
"Really Ceejai, you're going there?"
"Yes, I'm going there if it will knock some sense into your head! I don't want to see you get hurt over this!"
"You say hurt like Brianna wasn't killed!"
"I know Daddy got a little rough with her, but she brought it on herself, Nikki! You know that!"
"Brianna didn't deserve to die like that. I still can't believe Daddy's cover-up worked."
"Yeah, it worked and it's going to work again if you don't tell him that you're going to have this abortion."
"Daddy wouldn't hurt me, he loves me!"
"Girl, stop! Daddy loves his money more and no chick will get in the way of that. Shoot, he's coming back!
"What are you going to do, Nikki?"
"I'm not giving up my baby..."
"Then he's going to kill you!"
"Not if I run away first!"
"Stop playing games, Nikki! You know you won't be able to get away from him! Just have the abortion!
"NO! I'm not having an abortion!"
"So you're going to leave your sisters behind?"
"Our mom can look out for them! She always loved them more anyway!"
"What are you talking about? Okay, here he comes!"

"Alright ladies, time is up! Ceejai, were you able to talk some sense into your friend here?"
"Yes, Daddy I talked to her. She's going to take care of that little problem for you. Isn't that right Nikki?"

PASTOR'S ANNIVERSARY

PRESENT DAY

22-year-old Giovanni Ballard lives in Gainesville, Florida and has just recently graduated from the University of Florida (UF) with dual Bachelor's degrees in Accounting and Business. He's been accepted into the Masters program at the university where he plans to continue his studies in Accounting, Business and Finance. Growing up, Giovanni was not like the boys his age who typically played sports like football or basketball. Giovanni didn't mind playing those sports for fun with his friends, but he never had a desire to play in school. He always had an interest and fascination with numbers and even though Giovianni always made the honor roll, Math was his favorite subject. Giovanni grew up in Miami with his mother, Brianna Ballard and his four younger siblings: Nicholas, Asia, Kyle, and Chris. Giovanni grew up never knowing anything about his biological father or his mother's past. Anytime he would ask, Brianna would always tell him that it was best that he never who he was.

After several failed attempts of talking to his mother, Giovanni eventually stopped asking and he tried to get used to not having his father around or knowing anything about him. But some days were easier than others not having a father or any kind of male figure around to guide him. The only thing that Giovanni knew about his mother's life was that she was an exotic dancer because he remembered the times she would leave them home alone at night while she left to dance at the strip club and then come back home around three or four in the morning. Giovanni's best friend, Derrick lived across the hall with his mother and older sister. Usually when Brianna would leave in the middle of the night to dance at the club, Derrick's mother would come and check on them periodically until she came back home. Giovanni was almost eleven when his mother stopped dancing and started working at a grocery store to make ends meet. All of Brianna's decisions weren't perfect but she was determined to make sure that all five of her children did well in school so they could go to college, graduate and do something with their lives because she missed the opportunity to further her education. In spite of everything, Giovanni and his siblings made their mother proud by getting good grades in school and being on good behavior at all times. But Giovanni still wanted answers. He wanted to know who his father was and where he came from.

Even though Brianna maintained a job, she would drink a lot of alcohol and there were times where Giovanni could remember hearing his mother crying through her bedroom door late at night. He knew something had happened to her and that she couldn't talk about it, but he wanted the truth. Giovanni became desperate one day when he was at Derrick's house playing video games and he asked his mother if she knew anything about his dad or Brianna's past lifestyle. Outside of her dancing, the only thing that Derrick's mom knew was that she remembered Brianna moving into the apartment when she was still pregnant with him. She went on to explain that she was pregnant with Derrick around the same time and since she lived across the hall, they started talking and eventually became friends. Derrick and Giovanni were born two months apart which made Derrick's mother and Brianna grow even closer as friends. While Giovanni was happy that Derrick's mom told him some information about his mother, it wasn't enough. He wanted to know where she moved from and if she had been in Miami all of her life. He wanted to know if his father was in Miami or if he was somewhere else. Was he dead or alive? Questions that Giovanni deserved to have the answers to but as he got older, he felt that he would have to find those answers on his own and he had no idea on how he would go about doing that. The mystery remained when it came to Nicholas, Kyle and Asia's father because Brianna never wanted to answer questions about their father either. But it wasn't that way for Chris. Giovanni remembered seeing Brianna in a committed relationship with Chris' biological father, Chris, Sr. and how he treated Giovanni, Nicholas, Asia and Kyle like they were his own children. Giovanni thought life would be somewhat complete when Brianna found out she was pregnant with Chris. But early into their relationship when Chris was 5-years-old, things took a tragic turn for the worse.

One day Chris, Sr. walked a couple of streets over to his mother's house to pick Chris up after he spent a few hours with her and Chris, Sr's sisters and brothers who were visiting. After he picked Chris up and started walking back home, a black car with tinted windows pulled up alongside Chris, Sr. as he carried Chris in his arms after he had fallen asleep.

The driver of the vehicle rolled down the window and fired three shots at Chris, Sr. who immediately fell to the ground as he did his best to cover his son so he wouldn't be hit by the bullets. Chris, Sr. 's three older brothers weren't far from where Chris had been shot and they came running outside to see what happened after hearing the gunshots. His brothers found Chris, Sr. lying on the unground barely breathing with Chris lying in his arms crying and covered in his father's blood. One of the brothers picked him up to make sure he wasn't injured as the other two called for help. By the time the police and the paramedics arrived, it was too late. Chris, Sr. was dead. Once Chris had been medically cleared, he was returned home to Brianna and they did their best to move on without Chris, Sr. in their lives anymore.

Chris wasn't the same after that incident. He was having nightmares, crying spells and would sometimes wake up in the middle of the night screaming for his dad. Brianna did her best to comfort him but it wasn't enough. When Chris was 8-years-old, Giovanni found him in their bedroom on the floor bleeding out after he used a knife from the kitchen to slit his wrists multiple times. Giovanni remembered covering the wounds with his shirt while he screamed for his mother who was down the hall in her room. She panicked when she realized what Chris had done and she called the paramedics who came to their house and took Chris to the hospital. Giovanni was 16-years-old at the time and he was worried about what would happen to his brother after this incident. Chris was taken to a

behavioral health facility for youth and was treated
there by a therapist and a psychiatrist. It was the first
time that Chris had received any kind of counseling
since the day his father was killed.

Chris was diagnosed with Depression, Post
Traumatic Stress Disorder (PTSD), Anxiety Disorder,
Schizophrenia and Bipolar Disorder. Before he was
released to go home, he was placed on medication
that he was required to take once each day with
counseling once a week and a follow up with the
psychiatrist once every thirty days. Brianna stopped
working and received disability for Chris on top of
the money she was receiving in child support from
Asia and Nicholas' father who never came around or
spent time with Asia or Nicholas. Chris made good
grades but he was not in regular or honors classes, he
was placed in a school for children and youth with
behavioral problems. Giovanni hated it because he
knew how smart his brother was and that a school
like that would always limit his ability. But he also
knew there was nothing more he could do other than
to be there for him as much as he could. When
Giovanni got his acceptance into college, he almost
turned it down because he didn't know how Chris
would react to him leaving. Giovanni had never been
away from Chris for longer than a few hours, he
didn't know how he would respond to him leaving for
four years and only visiting on weekends and
holidays. To Giovanni's surprise, Chris took the news
about Giovanni going off to college much better than
he thought he would. Giovanni still remembered
what Chris said to him when he said where he was

going to school. Chris told Giovanni that he was going to go to the same school one day when he graduated and he wanted to study the same things he studied and do all of the same things he did.

Giovanni encouraged his brother by telling him that he could do anything he put his mind to. After that, Giovanni started spending more time with Chris by helping him with his studies and teaching him things that the school he was going to wouldn't teach him because they didn't think he was smart enough. Giovanni always knew how smart his brother was and hearing him say that he wanted to follow in his footsteps made him want to do whatever he could to help him accomplish that goal and do even better than he does. The work that Giovanni put in with Chris before he left for college paid off because Chris was able to test out of the school he was in and was allowed to skip a grade. He's 14-years-old and he's in the ninth grade taking honors classes for the first time in his life and beating every statistic that said he would never read at or above his grade level. Like Giovanni, Chris never took an interest in sports. He loved numbers and did great in Math just like Giovanni. When Giovanni got ready to leave for college at eighteen, Nicholas was 15-years-old, Asia was 14-years-old and Chris was 12-years-old. The three of them promised they would look out for Chris and help him with everything Giovanni had taught him so far since all three of them were good at Math and their other studies too.

Giovanni's best friend, Derrick was accepted into college at Florida A&M University in Tallahassee on a full scholarship that would allow him to play in the band. Giovanni and Derrick had been friends their entire lives and didn't think they would end up going two different paths with college. Derrick tried convincing Giovanni to come with him but Giovanni had a feeling come over him when he was deciding between the two schools. He didn't know why but he had this feeling that he was going to find answers when he got to Gainesville and made the tough decision of separating from Derrick to attend school there. Derrick was a little disappointed at first but he also knew how desperate Giovanni had been trying to get answers about his father and finding out more about his mother's past since Giovanni didn't know any other members from his family outside of his mother and younger siblings. Giovanni and Derrick remained friends and visited each other pretty regularly throughout college. Derrick graduated the same semester as Giovanni and he now has a 1-year-old son who his mother and older sister moved to Tallahassee to help him take care of after the child's mother died while giving birth to him.

Giovanni has been attending college the last four years not knowing that the answers he had been seeking for were much closer to him than he realized and he was going to eventually get those answers in a way he could have never anticipated. When Giovanni came to UF as a freshman, he met Preston Hampton who was a sophomore and his younger brother, Ramon who was the same age as Giovanni. The three of them clicked and instantly became friends who

lived in the same dorm. The same week they met,
Preston and Ramon introduced Giovanni to their
older brother, Pastor Titus Hampton who lived in a
house not far from the campus with his wife, Dianna.
Giovanni never grew up going to church or being
taught anything about God or the Bible, so he was
completely caught off guard when he realized Titus
was a pastor and that Ramon and Preston were saved
and leaders for the campus ministry organization at
their university.

Giovanni wasn't interested in becoming a part
of what they were doing at first because he wasn't
religious and didn't know anything about what they
believed nor did he have a real desire to learn. Once
Giovanni was honest with them about where he was,
he thought it was going to change things between
them but it didn't. They remained friends and even
spent time together off campus when they weren't in
class. Giovanni was surprised that they didn't give
him a hard time for not joining their club or going to
Titus' church that was designed to minister to college
students around his age. Giovanni was able to be
himself with Titus, Preston and Ramon and he never
felt pressured to believe the way they did. But things
changed for Giovanni the summer before he got
ready to start his sophomore year in one of the most
unlikely ways. While Giovanni was in Miami spending
time with his family for the summer, Titus and his
brothers came to visit him. When the four of them
went out to eat and see the city, Giovanni received a
frantic call from his mother who said that his brother,
Chris was having a manic episode after waking up

from a nightmare and she didn't know what to do
besides calling the police. Giovanni was comfortable
calling for help until they could get him to calm down
out of fear of how the police may respond to his
brother having an episode. He told his mom to have
Nicholas and Kyle hold him down until he got back to
the house.

Giovanni quickly drove back home as he
explained to Titus, Preston and Ramon what was
happening. At that moment, Giovanni felt a little
awkward about telling his friends about his brother's
condition because he had never mentioned it to them
before. It wasn't something Giovanni spoke much to
anyone about because he never wanted them to judge
his brother. When Giovanni arrived back at his mom's
apartment, he was going to have Titus, Preston and
Ramon wait in the car for him to come back while he
went to deal with Chris. But to his surprise, they
asked if they could come with him. Giovanni didn't
know exactly why they wanted to come with him
right then but he didn't have time to ask a bunch of
questions so he told them they could follow him to
the apartment not knowing that his life was about to
change forever. Giovanni walked inside the
apartment and saw that Chris was still having a panic
attack as Nicholas held him tightly in his arms while
their mom, Asia and Kyle tried to talk him down.
Giovanni rushed over to try and talk to Chris as he
continued crying and panicking, but it didn't seem to
be working this time. Brianna had already given Chris
his medication for the day so she didn't know what
else to do besides have him go to hospital and that

was when Titus walked over to where they were with
Preston and Ramon not far behind him. He asked
Brianna if he could pray for Chris. The request caught
everyone including Giovanni off guard. Giovanni and
his siblings looked at their mom to see what she
would say. It was obvious that Brianna was reluctant
about letting Titus pray for her son but she was
desperate and willing to do anything to get Chris to
calm down so they wouldn't have to send him back to
the hospital and she allowed Titus to pray for Chris.
Giovanni, Asia and Brianna stepped back as Titus got
closer to Chris who was still being held by Kyle and
Nicholas.

Titus knelt down in front of him and slowly
reached out to grab Chris' hands. Chris tried pulling
back from Titus at first until he heard Titus' voice and
he told Chris that it was okay because he could trust
him. Titus immediately began to pray for Chris and
when he called out all of the mental illnesses that he
had been diagnosed with, Giovanni and his family
were in complete shock because Giovanni had only
told Titus, Preston and Ramon that his brother
battled with mental illness. He never told him the
details or what he was diagnosed with. As Titus
continued praying while he held Chris' hands, Chris
finally started to come down from the anxiety attack
he was having until Kyle and Nichole were able to
loosen their grip of Chris who immediately jumped
into Titus' arms as he Titus finished praying for him.
Giovanni and his family couldn't believe what they
were seeing because Chris was usually never that
open to anyone he didn't know. Chris embraced Titus

as Titus held him in his arms and said words of
encouragement in his ear before slowly sitting him
back down on the sofa between Kyle and Nicholas
who were still sitting on the sofa in awe of what had
just happened.

Brianna thanked Titus for praying for Chris
and helping him to calm down and rest peacefully.
Giovanni drove back to campus with Titus, Ramon
and Preston still in shock about what happened and
he told them about how they didn't grow up in
church at all and he was surprised that his mom
allowed Titus to pray for Chris the way he did. By the
end of that year, Brianna called Giovanni excited
because Chris' condition had improved
tremendously! So much so that he no longer needed
the medication he was taking and he took the tests
needed to get back into regular school and passed
with flying colors! Not only would be going back to
regular school with kids his age, but he would be in
honors classes. Giovanni broke down in tears when
his mother told him the news that day and before
Giovanni knew it, he was crying out to God and
thanking him for healing his brother from the trauma
he experienced when he was young and helping him
to excel in school. Giovanni was in his dorm room
alone while Ramon had gone down the hall to his
brothers' room to get something that he left behind.
When Ramon came back, he saw Giovanni on his
knees calling on the name of Jesus as tears fell from
his face. Ramon smiled with excitement as he quickly
ran back down the hall to grab Titus and Preston who
came to their dorm room to see what Ramon was

telling them. Titus got down on the floor with Giovanni and placed his arm around him as Preston and Ramon closed the door behind them and began to pray to themselves as Titus started to minister to Giovanni. He asked him what happened and wanted to know more about what he was feeling. Giovanni began telling them what had been happening with Chris since the beginning of the summer when he prayed for him at their house and he went on to explain that his brother was no longer taking medication and he was able to test back into regular school and was now taking honors classes.

In tears, Giovanni told Titus and his brothers that he knew God was real after witnessing the transformation with his brother and he wanted to get to know God and experience him the way they do. He told Titus that he didn't know what to do or where to start but he was ready to do anything to have God in his life. Titus, Ramon and Preston were in tears as Giovanni shared what was on his heart because the three of them had been praying for Giovanni to receive Jesus Christ into his life. Titus led him in the prayer of salvation and Giovanni gave his life to the Lord at that moment and his life had not been the same since. A couple of months after Giovanni gave his life to the Lord, he found the courage to tell his mother and his siblings. Giovanni knew his mother never took them to church or ever talked about God, so he wasn't surprised when she told him with tears in his eyes that he would one day regret his decision because God didn't love him the way he thought. Giovanni could hear the pain in her voice and he couldn't help but wonder if her past experiences were tied to the church and it made him want to get answers even more. It's now been three years since Giovanni gave his life to the Lord and he continues to live for God and he prays daily that his family will come to know God for themselves.

Giovanni had just returned back to Gainesville with Preston and Ramon after going to Atlanta to visit his sister, Asia who was now living there with two of her friends. She dropped out of school when she turned eighteen and is now working at the strip club making thousands of dollars a night as a dancer. Giovanni was shocked when he first found out that Asia decided to quit high school and move to Atlanta to become a dancer.

He couldn't understand how someone as smart as Asia could abruptly make a decision like this and he went to Atlanta to talk to her and find out what was really going on with her. Giovanni and Asia spent time together but he couldn't really get her to open up. She cried a few times, she even allowed Giovanni to pray for her and her two roommates but she wouldn't talk to him about why she felt the need to make this decision. Before leaving, Giovanni assured Asia that he was praying for her and that he was here to support her and that she didn't have to be afraid to talk to him about what was going on. It was Thursday morning as Giovanni rested in bed after coming back from his trip on Tuesday. He was getting ready to start his new job at a local bank in a couple of weeks so he wanted to spend as much time as possible relaxing before going to work. As Giovanni laid in his bed, he received a text message from his brother, Nicholas who is now a freshman at the university where he attends on a basketball scholarship. Giovanni looked at the message and it said that Nicholas was at his front door with a surprise for him. Giovanni sighed and shook his head because he thought his brother was playing a prank on him. But when he got to the door and opened it, he was in shock when he saw Asia standing at the door next to him with her duffel bag.

"Asia?" he asked, surprised.

"Look who I saw getting out of her car when I got here, bro!" Nicholas said, excitedly as Giovanni invited Nicholas and Asia inside of his apartment.

"Asia, are you okay?" Giovanni asked, concerned as they hugged each other.

"I'm okay. I know you just left Atlanta but I realized after you left that I do need to talk to you and I think I'm ready to tell you what I've been dealing with." Asia said as Giovanni smiled a little and nodded.

"How long are you going to stay?" Giovanni asked as they walked into the living room.

"Well, I took a few days off. Can I hang out here until Sunday?" she asked as Nicholas put Asia's bag in the guest room.

"Yeah, that's fine." Giovanni said as they sat on the sofa while Nicholas was in the kitchen drinking orange juice and talking on his cell phone.

"Bro, I know you didn't drink all of my juice!" Giovanni said as Nicholas sat across from them.

"Sorry Gio, I was thirsty!" Nicholas said as he and Asia started laughing.

"Don't you have class?" Asia asked.

"Not for a couple of hours." Nicholas replied as Giovanni shook his head.

"So do you need Nicholas to get out of here while we talk?" Giovanni asked.

"No, he can stay. I probably should tell you both." Asia told him.

"I'm out of orange juice but I have apple juice, tea and water if you want something to drink." Giovanni said.

"I'm okay for now, but thank you." Asia replied.

"You're welcome. So what's going on?" Giovanni asked as Asia sighed and paused for a moment before responding.

"I know this may be hard to believe but I've always felt like Mom wishes I was a boy." Asia said as Giovanni and Nicholas glanced at each other in shock at what she told them.

"What? Asia, why would you say that? Mom loves all of us." Giovanni said.

"No, she loves you, Nicholas, Kyle and Chris. She treats me like I disgust her, always has. I got tired of it and that's why I left the way I did. Kyle and Chris were so upset and I did my best to comfort them before I left, but I couldn't stay any longer. I had been waiting for this day." Asia told them.

"How long had you been planning to leave?" Giovanni asked.

"Since sixth grade. I knew if I left before, Mom would call the police and they would have to find me because I was a minor. But I knew that once I turned eighteen, nothing could be done. My two friends that you met wanted to do the same so we had been planning to go to Atlanta when we turned eighteen." Asia said as Giovanni paused for a moment before responding.

"Asia, have you ever tried talking to Mom and telling her what you told us?" Giovanni asked.
"Yeah, I tried that. It didn't work. She slapped me." Asia told them as Giovanni and Nicholas glanced at each other in shock.
"She slapped you? When? I don't remember that!" Nicholas said.
"Yeah, me either!" Giovanni replied.
"Gio, you had just left for college and the rest of you weren't home. It was one of the times you went outside to play basketball with the other guys." Asia said as tears fell from her face and Giovanni handed her tissue.
"Sis, I'm sorry about that. I didn't know that happened." Giovanni told her as he grabbed her hand.
"Yeah, me too sis." Nicholas added.
"Thank you. But now do you see why I wanted to get away from her? But you know what? Mom hasn't told us anything about her past, where she came from or anything about our biological fathers. But I feel like she hinted at it the night before I left for Atlanta." Asia said as Giovanni and Nicholas' expression changed.

"What do you mean, Asia?" Giovanni asked.

"Mom saw me packing and she asked me where I was going and I told her I was moving to Atlanta with my two best friends to start a new life. I won't lie, I thought Mom was going to hit me like she did before but she didn't." Asia said.

"What did she do?" Giovanni asked.

"She started crying and then she walked up next to me and said that if I wanted to go to Atlanta to be another slut on a pole then I should just do it, because it would only be a matter of time before I ended up just like her. She said it would only be a matter of weeks before I'm sold to the highest bidder, just like she was at my age." Asia glanced at her brothers who were totally caught off guard by what Asia told them.

"Mom said all of that to you?" Giovanni asked as Asia nodded.

"Yeah, she said every word and I'll never forget it because even though I had no idea what she was talking about, I knew she meant it and I knew that it had something to do with whatever happened to her in the past. So I asked her if Atlanta was her hometown and she wouldn't answer me. She told me to stop asking so many questions before she stormed out of my room and slammed the door behind her. It's crazy because I wasn't even thinking about stripping before she said what she said to me that night before I left." Asia said.

"But you did it anyway, Asia. Why?" Nicholas asked, confused.

"I guess it was my way of connecting to our mom in a way I never had before so I started working at the club with my friends. The club owner is older so I showed him a picture of my mom and asked him if he knew her and he said he didn't. But I didn't believe him." Asia said.

"What? Why?" Giovanni asked.

"He stared at her picture too long when I asked if he knew her and he gave this smirk. I didn't bother him about it because I didn't want him to fire me on the first night but guys, I think Mom is from Atlanta and I think she was a dancer." Asia said as Nicholas and Giovanni reacted to what she said.

"Are you serious? But you would have to be at least eighteen to work at the club and Mom was in Miami pregnant with me at eighteen." Giovanni said.

"How do you know that?" Asia asked.

"Derrick's mom told me one time when I was in middle school and went to their house to play video games. She didn't know a lot but I do remember her saying that my mom moved into the apartment we grew up in when she was eighteen and pregnant with me. Derrick's mom was around the same age as our mom and she was pregnant with him at the time. That's how they became friends." Giovanni said as Nicholas and Asia paused for a moment before responding.

"How far along was our mom when she got to Miami?" Nicholas asked as Giovanni shrugged his shoulders.

"Derrick's mom didn't say. Why?" Giovanni asked.

"Depending on how many months along Mom was when she got to Miami, isn't it possible that she was still a minor when she had sex?" Nicholas asked.

"Dang, that's possible. I didn't even think about it. I mean, I'm guessing she had a boyfriend or something who bailed on her once he found out she was pregnant. But I don't know because my mom has never told me anything about my father. She only confirmed that none of us have the same father but that's it." Giovanni said.

"That's crazy. We deserve to know the truth." Asia replied.

"You're right, we do and I've been trying to get answers for us for the last four years. That's why I came here instead of going to school with Derrick." Giovanni replied as Asia and Nicholas' expression changed.

"You know I never did ask you why you and Derrick didn't go to the same college. You chose to come here because you thought you would find answers? Mom hasn't been to Gainesville has she?" Nicholas asked.

"No, I don't think she has but I don't know, I just had this feeling. But I'll say this, I don't know about Atlanta but I do think Mom may have been a dancer here in Miami." Giovanni said.

"Are you serious? Why do you think that?" Asia asked.

"I was little at the time but I remember nights where I stayed up and would peep my head out my room door when Mom would come home late. I remember the clothes she would wear like high heel shoes, fishnet stockings, short skirts, halter tops and stuff like that." Giovanni said.

"Bro for real?" Nicholas asked as Giovanni nodded.

"Yeah, but I never knew for sure so I didn't say anything to you guys about it. Derrick's mom said our mom moved here from out of town but she never knew where. So obviously my biological father isn't here in Florida but yours probably is." Giovanni said.

"So you're going to help us find our dad too?" Asia asked.

"I will if that's what you want. But I strongly feel like the answers we all want will come once I can get answers about my own father first and find out exactly what our mom came through. Asia, you may have gotten me off to a good start." Giovanni said.

"Really?" Asia asked.

"Yeah, I think you have. The manager you confronted, what's his name?" Giovanni asked as he grabbed a pen and paper to write on.

"Hold on a minute, Gio! You're not going to call him or something are you?" Asia asked.

"No, I'm not going to call him. I just want to have a record of it while I search." Giovanni said.

"Okay, please don't get me fired. But his name is Jarvis Coleman, Sr. and he has three sons that work at the club too." Asia said as Giovanni wrote it down.

"Are his sons my age?" Giovanni asked.

"Oh no, they're much older. Jarvis, Jr. goes by "J.J" and he's in his early thirties along with his younger brother, Byron. Jarvis' youngest son, Lamar is in his mid to late twenties based on appearance." Asia replied as Giovanni nodded and continued writing.

"Okay sis, thank you." Giovanni said.

"So bro, you've been out here four years and you don't have any answers?" Nicholas asked as Giovanni sighed and shook his head.

"No, not yet. But the more I pray, the closer I feel that I am to getting it." Giovanni said.

"I still can't believe you're all in the church now." Asia said as Nicholas and Giovanni laughed a little.

"Sometimes I can't believe it myself but I'm here. I still pray for you two, Chris and Mom to experience God the way I have for yourselves." Giovanni said.

"Bro, that's not happening! Have you seen these freshmen girls out here? I don't know how you stayed so strong!" Nicholas replied as Giovanni and Asia started laughing athis response.

"Sex isn't everything, Nicholas." Giovanni replied.

"Man, you're just saying that because you found the Lord." Nicholas said.

"Bro, I'm serious. You're on the football team and practically a celebrity now. These girls would love to ruin all of that for you by trapping you with a baby. Watch your step and don't sleep with everything in a skirt. I would just tell you to wait until you're married but I know you won't listen so at least be careful and be selective." Giovanni said.

"I will. I mean, did that happen to someone?" Nicholas asked.

"Yeah, it happened to one guy. He came onto the team freshman year just like you when I got here. Name was everywhere and he was the big man on campus. Then I suddenly stopped seeing his face on the news, they weren't doing articles about him or anything. It turned out he was about to become a father and as soon as his coach found out, they kicked him off the team." Giovanni said as Nicholas looked shocked.

"Are you serious? He was kicked off the team because he got a girl pregnant?" Nicholas asked, surprised.

"Honestly, there were rumors that he was kicked off but I also heard he quit and left school. But I don't know for sure. I just heard the coaches have strict rules. I mean, you've been there for a semester so far, are they strict?" Giovanni asked as Nicholas nodded.

"Yeah, they're pretty strict but I didn't think anything like that happened. Don't worry about me bro, I'll be good." Nicholas said as he and Giovanni slapped hands.

"So where are you planning to get these answers, Gio? I mean, maybe you should snoop around Miami or Atlanta since mom has no ties to Gainesville." Asia said.

"I know but I don't feel I'm supposed to go just yet." Giovanni said as Nicholas reacted to something he was looking at on his phone.

"What is it, Nicholas?" Asia asked as Nicholas walked over and sat closer to them.

"Gio, look at this!" Nicholas said, handing Giovanni his phone.

"What? Who is this?" Giovanni asked.

"I don't know how I'm just now noticing her but she's a freshman on the women's basketball team here on campus. Look, her last name is Ballard just like us! Do you think we could be related?" Nicholas asked.

"I mean, I guess that's always possible and she's right around you and Asia's age too." Giovanni said as Asia took a look.

"Jasmine Ballard. You didn't see her around last semester?" Asia asked, glancing at Nicholas.

"No, I didn't pay attention to her. I really don't follow the girls' team. Bro, should I ask her where she's from and about her people?" Nicholas asked.

"That might catch her off guard if you do that so not right now. Now if she asks you anything, talk to her and tell me anything she says. She's probably going to hear about you at some point if she hasn't already. But don't ask her anything right now and just in case we are related, don't date her." Giovanni said.

"I won't, don't worry. It's not every day you meet someone with our same last name." Nicholas replied as Giovanni nodded.

Nicholas left Giovanni's apartment shortly after and headed back to campus to attend his next class while Giovanni showered and got ready to meet up with Titus, Ramon and Preston. Asia wanted to rest for a while after the long drive so Giovanni gave her his spare key to use before leaving the apartment and heading to Titus' house to eat lunch which was being prepared by Titus' wife, Dianna. As Giovanni drove to his house, he thought about the conversation he just finished having with Asia and Nicholas about their mom. He was more determined now than ever to keep searching for answers not knowing that the answers he was searching for were much closer to him than he realized. Giovanni stopped at the gas station to fill up his tank and as he stood outside of his car, he received a text message from Nicholas and it caught him off guard. Nicholas told Giovanni that when he walked on campus and headed to his class, he saw Ramon and Preston in a hallway nearby talking to Jasmine Ballard. Giovanni replied and asked if he was sure it was Jasmine since he knew Nicholas had only seen a picture of Jasmine so far. Nicholas replied and said he was positive because she was wearing a tank-top that had her jersey number on the front and her last name on the back of it as she turned to walk away from them after they finished talking. Nicholas and Giovanni were both shocked at the fact that they knew who Jasmine was when she's an incoming freshman and that both of them had already graduated. Giovanni told Nicholas not to worry and that he would get to the bottom of it since he was getting ready to meet up with them. Giovanni sent a text message to Titus and said he would be running about fifteen minutes late because he had to go back to his apartment before he came to see them. After Giovanni left the gas station, he drove to the store to pick up items he knew Asia liked and took them back to his apartment so she would have food to eat once she woke up. Asia was sound asleep in his guest room so he left her a note under a cell phone instead of waking her up.

Giovanni quickly left his apartment again and drove as fast as he could to Titus' house hoping Ramon and Preston would be there. His timing was perfect because Ramon and Preston were pulling into the driveway as Giovanni arrived at Titus' house. The three of them greeted each other as they walked up the steps and headed inside the house after Titus opened the door for them. Giovanni didn't know how to ask Ramon and Preston about his conversation with Jasmine without sounding weird, but he was going to head home until they told him why they were talking to Jasmine and how they knew her. About ten minutes later, the food was ready and the five of them ate at the dining room table. About twenty minutes later, Dianna kissed Titus and said goodbye to them before leaving to meet with a client she had an appointment with, leaving Giovanni to talk with Titus, Ramon and Preston. They were having a great conversation as usual and Giovanni just couldn't figure out when he should ask Ramon and Preston about their conversation with Jasmine. He took a deep breath and decided to bring it up because he didn't know if there would ever be a right time.

"Guys, I need to ask you something." Giovanni said as they finished eating.

"What's going on, Giovanni?" Preston asked.

"Nicholas texted me on my way here and said he saw you and Ramon near his class talking to Jasmine Ballard, the freshman on the women's basketball team. How do you know her?" Giovanni asked as Preston, Ramon and Titus glanced at each other in shock at what Giovanni told them.

"I keep forgetting that your brother, Nicholas is here now on a basketball scholarship too. Had we remembered that we would have been a little more discreet about where we had our conversation." Ramon said.

"I mean, I'm not even saying it's that big of a deal. I'm just curious because Nicholas, Asia and I were talking about her right before I left home to come see you guys." Giovanni said.

"You were? Wait, you know her too?" Preston asked.

"No, we don't know her. Nicholas ran across something online and when he saw that Jasmine had the same last name as us, he wondered if it was possible that we were related. I told him I wasn't sure but I made a note of it because I'm still on the search to find out my history and where I come from since my mom wouldn't answer my questions." Giovanni said.

"Yeah, I meant to ask you about that, Giovanni. How has your search been going? Are you any closer to finding out anything? Has your mom opened up?" Titus asked.

"My mom hasn't opened up about anything and before my sister dropped in on me today, I was really running out of ideas." Giovanni said as Preston's expression changed.

"Your sister, Asia? She's here?" Preston asked.

"Oh yeah, I'm sorry. She showed up at my doorstep today. She drove here to talk to me and open up about some things. What she told me wasn't a whole lot but it was a start." Giovanni replied as Titus, Ramon and Preston glanced at each other again.

"Giovanni, if you don't mind, can you tell us what Asia told you?" Titus asked as Giovanni took another sip of his drink.

"Oh yeah, I can. It wasn't much though. So Asia started off by telling me why she dropped out of high school when she turned eighteen with her two best friends and took off to Atlanta. Her reasoning had to do with how she was feeling about our mom and how she felt our mom felt about her. As we continued talking, Asia said that our mom made this statement to her the night before she left that made her wonder if she was ever a dancer and if he had any ties to Atlanta as far as her childhood was concerned. When she started working at the strip club, she showed our mom's picture to her boss to see if he by chance knew who she was since he was older and had been the owner of the club for several years." Giovanni said.

"She did? What did he say?" Titus asked.

"Asia said that he told her he didn't know her but she couldn't help but wonder if he was telling the truth or not because he stared at our mom's picture a good minute before he said anything at all. Asia didn't want to get fired so she didn't push the issue but I thought the information she did gather might help me with what I'm trying to find out so I asked her to give me his name and she did." Giovanni said as Titus glanced at Preston and Ramon again.

"Giovanni, you said you wrote his name down? What was it?" Titus asked as Giovanni pulled his tablet out of his backpack to look at what he wrote down.

"Oh, here it is! Asia said his name was Jarvis Coleman, Sr. She said his three older sons: J.J, Byron and Lamar work at the club too. Why?" Giovanni asked as Titus sighed, glanced at his brothers and paused for a moment before responding. "What is it?"

"I can't believe this. I guess we're going to have to tell you everything sooner than we were planning to now." Titus said as Giovanni looked confused.

"Tell me everything about what? What are you guys talking about? You still haven't answered my original question about Jasmine Ballard." Giovanni said.

"Titus, we don't have to tell him yet do we?" Ramon asked.

"Yeah, we need to do it because now I know why Mom sent me that weird text I told you two about the other day." Titus glanced at Ramon and Preston who reacted to what he said.

"Oh my God, you're right bro! That's why! He got shook when he saw the picture, right?" Ramon asked as Giovanni looked even more confused.

"Will someone tell me what's going on here? What are you talking about?" Giovanni asked, sternly as Titus got up from his seat at the head of the table and walked over to sit next to Giovanni.

"Giovanni, we need to tell you something that may upset you because we didn't tell you when we met you four years ago. But we've waited all this time for a reason." Titus said.

"I don't understand, Titus. What do you need to tell me?" Giovanni asked.

"Giovanni, do you remember what I told you I was going to prepare you for after you first got saved?" Titus asked.

"Yeah, you said God wanted to use me to be a voice and that you, Preston and Ramon were going to help me get ready and have the boldness it would take to one day speak for God and others. I didn't fully know what that meant, but I trusted you so I didn't ask. But what does that have to do with anything right now?" Giovanni asked.

Before Titus could respond, Giovanni's phone started ringing and he initially ignored the call

without looking at the screen because he wanted to
hear what Titus was going to say next. But the phone
started ringing again and Giovanni could hear
multiple text messages coming through on his phone
so he decided to look to see who it was. To his
surprise, the missed calls were from his mother and
the text messages were from Asia who was begging
Giovanni to come back to his apartment because
their mom had just shown up there unexpectedly
with Chris. She was in tears and it was clear that she
was terrified about something but Asia couldn't figure
out what it was because Brianna wouldn't talk. She
just kept asking for Giovanni and she said she would
talk once she saw Giovanni. Giovanni didn't know
what was going on but he knew he needed to get
back home as quickly as he could. He replied to Asia's
text and told her to tell their mom she was on the
way. He told Asia to set their mom up in his other
guest room inside the apartment and they would
figure out the rest when he got back.

Giovanni quickly started packing up his things
as he explained to Titus, Ramon and Preston what
was going on and he told them that even though he
really wanted to finish their conversation, he needed
to go see what was wrong because his mom wouldn't
just show up like this if something wasn't up. As
Giovanni got ready to leave, Titus asked if he, Ramon
and Preston could come with him and Giovanni said
they could. Titus sent a message to his wife to let her
know where he was going and he promised to be
home later on as Giovanni and Ramon got into his car
while Titus and Preston followed behind him in their

car to Giovanni's apartment. As Giovanni started driving down the street, he handed his cell phone to Ramon and asked him to send a text message to Nicholas telling him that their mom and Chris were at his apartment. He went on to explain that he wasn't sure what was going on but he knew it had to be serious for their mom to just show up like this. Nicholas replied and said that he wouldn't be able to come to his apartment until around seven or eight tonight because he had practice this afternoon and couldn't miss it.

When Giovanni stopped at another red light, he replied to Nicholas and told him it was okay and that he would fill him in on what was going on later. As Giovanni continued driving, he remembered that the only reason Kyle didn't come with them was because he was at basketball camp and wouldn't be back for a few weeks. About fifteen minutes later: Giovanni, Ramon, Titus and Preston arrived at his apartment and they quickly got out of their cars and started walking to the second floor where his apartment was. Giovanni noticed his mom's car as they were walking by and he noticed that it was packed with a lot of stuff as if she was moving or something and it didn't make any sense to him. As they stopped at the door and waited for Giovanni to open his apartment with his key, they could hear Brianna and Asia arguing. As the four of them walked inside, that was when Brianna slapped Asia across her face causing her to fall to the floor.

"Mama, calm down! Relax!" Giovanni said as he quickly ran over to grab his mother and pull her away from Asia as she attempted to kick her while she was on the floor crying hysterically.

"Let me go, Giovanni! This is all her fault!" Brianna said, enraged as Preston closed and locked the door while Ramon and Titus helped Asia up off the floor and walked her over to the sofa where Chris was sitting.

"Hey Titus!" Chris said, excitedly as he jumped up and ran into Titus' arms, hugging him tightly as Titus smiled and embraced him.

"Hey Chris, how are you? You still remember me?" he asked.

"Yeah, I remember you! You prayed for me! Mom said you were the reason why I got better!" Chris said as Titus laughed a little.

"Well Chris, it was God who healed you. He just used me in the moment to make it happen. Your brother told me how well you've been doing, I'm proud of you." Titus replied as Chris hugged him again.

"Thank you so much, Titus!" Chris replied.

"I don't know if Chris needs to hear what we're about to talk about right now. Giovanni, where's Nicholas?" Brianna asked as he handed her and Asia some water to drink.

"We probably won't see him until tonight, he's still on campus and has practice this afternoon." Giovanni said as Brianna sighed and shook her head as she glanced at Chris sitting next to Titus.

"I really don't want him to hear this." Brianna replied.

"Ms. Ballard, did you want one of us to take Chris outside until you guys were done talking?" Preston asked as Brianna paused for a moment before responding.

"What were your last names?" Brianna asked as Titus, Ramon and Preston's expression changed.

"Hampton." Titus replied as Brianna nodded.

"Mom, I thought I told you that." Giovanni said.

"I don't remember, I just needed to see for myself since it's been a while since I've seen them. I couldn't figure out why the three of you looked so familiar that day you were at my apartment and you prayed for my son. But now I'm starting to connect the dots. Titus, Preston and Ramon Hampton. Right?" Brianna asked as Giovanni and Asia glanced at each other, still confused.

"Yes Mama, that's their name. Why is this a big deal?" Giovanni asked as Brianna glanced at him and tears fell from her face.

"Chris, go chill in Gio's room until we're done, okay?" Asia asked as Chris nodded and headed down the hall to where Giovanni's room was and closed the door behind him.

"Mama, you're scaring me right now. Can you please tell me what's going on and why you showed up here with Chris in a panic? And why were you and Brianna fighting?" Giovanni asked as Brianna pulled a chair up and sat down while Giovanni sat on the table near the sofa where Asia, Titus, Preston and Ramon were sitting.

"I know who the three of you are. I remember. You're Eddie & Felicia Hampton's boys aren't you?" Brianna said, still glancing at Titus, Preston and Ramon.

"What? You know their parents?" Giovanni asked, shocked.

"Yes ma'am…"

"So you haven't told Giovanni the truth? I mean Titus, if Giovanni is 22-years-old then you're about 30-years-old now right? So you have to know." Brianna said as Giovanni glanced at them wondering what his mom was talking about.

"Brianna, we were waiting for the right time to tell Giovanni the truth and believe it or not, we were about to do just that when he was at my house just now. But then you called him and he rushed back here to see you." Titus said.

"Hello? I'm standing right here! Can someone tell me what's going on? What are you guys talking about?" Giovanni asked, sternly.

"Hold on Giovanni, we're about to fill you in. So you three were going to drop a bombshell that big on my son without talking to his mother first? Why didn't you say something to me three years ago when you came to my house?" Brianna asked.

"Brianna, we're sorry, okay? You looked familiar to us too that day and when Giovanni introduced you to us, our mouths almost dropped because we thought you were dead." Titus said.

"I'm trying to figure out how you know about any of this considering how young you were when this went down! Ramon, you weren't even born yet! I remember because your mom found out she was pregnant with you around the same time I found out I was pregnant with Giovanni." Brianna said.

"You're right Brianna, Ramon wasn't born yet. Preston and I were kids, but we weren't stupid. We could see and we remembered when the detectives showed up at our dad's church investigating a girl named Brianna's death because her family didn't think it was an accident." Titus said.

"But when we met you that day, we went back and looked at our dad's files again and we realized that the Brianna we were thinking of was Brianna Harris, not Brianna Ballard." Preston said.

"Right, and that was when I looked at everything again and realized what the note in the file by your name meant when it said *the girl who got away*." I had no idea what he meant by that until we looked at the file again." Titus said.

"Okay, for real! What the hell's going on? What do you mean you thought my mom was dead? You're saying that like you've known her the whole time or something!" Giovanni said, still confused about what they were talking about as Brianna glanced at Asia and shook her head.

"Let me talk first, guys. Thanks to this nosey daughter of mine, I have to tell you something I was planning to carry to the grave. Thanks to this nosey daughter of mine, everything I've done over the years to hide and keep my children safe went down the drain because of YOU!" Brianna said, enraged as she pointed and looked at Asia who was sitting on the sofa wiping her tears with the tissue Giovanni gave her.

"Mama, I'm sorry. I didn't know." Asia said.

"Didn't know what, Asia?" Giovanni asked as Asia attempted to respond and Brianna stopped her.

"I will slap you again if you say anything else, Asia. You've talked enough! But before I start talking, what made you show him my picture?" Brianna asked.

"It was what you said the night before I left. I wasn't even thinking about stripping and when you made that statement, it made me wonder if it was something you did once before in Atlanta. When you didn't answer my question after I asked you if Atlanta was your hometown, I thought I would be like Giovanni and search for answers too. So when me and my friends started dancing at the club, we noticed the manager was much older and I figured if you were ever a dancer, he would know so I showed him the picture. But he said he didn't know you so I didn't think it was a big deal." Asia said.

"I don't really know where your brother was looking for answers, but wherever he was looking didn't almost get me killed!" Brianna said as tears fell from her face again.

"Mama, talk to me, please! What's going on?" Giovanni asked as he grabbed her hand and Brianna turned her attention from Brianna and faced him.

"Because of what your sister did and what happened today, I have to tell you what you've been

wanting to know for the last 22 years of your life."
Brianna said as Giovanni's expression changed.

"What? So you're going to finally tell me who
my dad is and where you came from?" Giovanni asked
as Brianna nodded.

"Yes, I'm going to tell you. I don't have a choice
at this point." Brianna said.

"Okay Mama, I'm listening. Tell me
everything!" Giovanni replied as Brianna sighed and
nodded.

"Asia's suspicions were right, I was born and
raised in Atlanta, Georgia. I never knew who my
father was, it was just me, my mom, Veronica Ballard,
my three younger sisters: Lauren, Kristen and Tia
Ballard. My mother was an evangelist so we were
always at church. Growing up, I always saw how
many teens from our church were sending off with
full four year scholarships to college not knowing
what the teenage girls were having to do to get those
scholarships." Brianna said.

"They were doing something different from
the boys? Is that what you mean, Mama?" Giovanni
asked as Brianna nodded.

"Yes, that's right. When I turned thirteen, I
joined a group of girls that were around my age, some
a couple of years older than me. My mom said we
were in a club that was going to allow us to get those
same kinds of scholarships when we were seniors
getting ready for college. She said all we had to do
was keep our grades up and I did. But I soon found

out there was more to it than that, much more." Brianna said.

"What happened?" Giovanni asked.

"Since the girls in the group were very developed, the pastor and his wife knew that with the right hair, make-up and clothing, we could pass for eighteen to the high paying men that came to one of the popular strip clubs in Atlanta. It's the one you work at Asia." Brianna said as Asia reacted to what she said.

"Oh my God, it is?" Asia asked.

"Yeah, it is." Brianna replied as she turned her attention back to Giovanni. "Twice a month on Friday nights, we had to dance in the VIP rooms for men old enough to be our dad and even grandfathers at times. Most of the time, we were doing all kind of sexual favors for the pastor and sometimes his wife would join in too." Brianna said as Titus, Ramon and Preston did their best to remain their composure as Brianna talked about their parents.

"Mama, wait a minute. This went on and your mom knew nothing about it? Did your sisters have to do it too?" Giovanni asked, disgusted at what he was hearing.

"Yeah, their time eventually came too and yes, my mother knew about everything!" Brianna replied.

"Why didn't she do anything to save you? Why didn't she call the police?" Giovanni asked, still in shock as Brianna laughed sarcastically.

"Oh no, no one was going to call the police unless they wanted to risk missing out on their perks." Brianna replied.

"Perks? What kind of perks?" Giovanni asked.

"All of the girls in this group came from single parent households with mothers who didn't have support from any of their kids' fathers. So they were desperate and willing to do anything to have money to do whatever they wanted and not have to work a nine to five." Brianna said.

"So your pastor was paying your mom to stay quiet and allow this to happen to you and your sisters?" Giovanni asked.

"See, I knew you with your degree you would catch on. That's exactly what happened. So my mom knew what was going on." Brianna said.

"Mama, I don't mean to sound funny when I ask this but you didn't like this did you?" Giovanni asked.

"I didn't at first. I knew I should not have been having sex with my pastor, a man old enough to be my father and the same man who promised my mom that he would look out for us. But a few drinks and pills into it, you become numb. You don't feel it anymore, you just go with it." Brianna said.

"They drugged you and got you drunk?" Giovanni asked.

"Yes, they did. I was popping pills and drinking like crazy all the way up to my senior year of high school. A week after my eighteenth birthday, I got the shock of my life when my period came late. I knew from a sex education class I took freshman year that a missed period could potentially mean I was pregnant but I didn't want to believe that was the case. So I tried to let it slide for a while but after a week of no period, I told my best friend, Ceejai." Brianna said.

"You told your best friend instead of Grandma?" Giovanni asked.

"No, my mom would have beat the crap out of me if I would have told her my period was late so I told Ceejai. We were both seniors in high school that year, months away from getting our money. Ceejai panicked when I told her I was late. We got on the bus and went to the store to get a pregnancy test and I took it at her house while her mom was out." Brianna said.

"That was when you realized you were pregnant with me, right?" Giovanni asked as Brianna nodded with more tears welling up into her eyes.

"Yes, that's right. I was pregnant." Brianna said as Giovanni did his best to maintain his composure and not start crying with her.

"Mama, thank you. I know you've said a lot so far and yes, I want to know it all. But if you need time, we can stop for a minute." Giovanni said as Brianna shook her head and kissed Giovanni on his forehead.

"Thank you, but I need to get this out so I'm going to keep talking." Brianna said.

"Okay Mama, that's fine. So you found out you were pregnant. Was your boyfriend the father?" Giovanni asked.

"I didn't have a boyfriend..."

"Okay, so it was just a boy from school you hooked up with that got you pregnant?" Giovanni asked as Brianna shook her head.

"No, it wasn't a boy from school or even a boy my age. I missed a couple of times with my birth control and the only person I was sexually active with at the time was my pastor, Eddie Hampton." Brianna said as Giovanni looked surprised.

"What? Your pastor got you pregnant? That's who my father is?" Giovanni asked in shock.

"Yes, that's right." Brianna said as Giovanni shook his head and thought for a moment before responding. He paused and then glanced over at Titus, Preston and Ramon who were sitting on the sofa next to Asia in tears.

"No! No way! Hampton?" Giovanni asked as he started to panic and Brianna tried to calm him down as he broke down in tears and Titus, Preston and Ramon walked over to him.

"Calm down, baby. I'm sorry. I am so sorry." Brianna said as Giovanni pulled away from her and looked at the four of them.

"Giovanni, it's okay. We're here for you." Titus said as Giovanni backed up against the wall still crying as Asia walked over to stand next to him.

"Oh my God, I can't believe this! So wait, that's how you know each other? Pastor Hampton is your father?" Giovanni asked.

"Yes Giovanni, that's right. He's our father and you're our half-brother." Titus said as Giovanni panicked again.

"Wait a minute! You knew we were brothers the whole time we've been friends and you didn't tell me? How could you keep that a secret all this time?" Giovanni asked, sternly.

"Giovanni, please don't be mad at Preston or Ramon. They wanted to tell you the moment we realized your mom was not the girl who's death the police were investigating. But I told them we were going to wait until you had grown enough in your walk with God to tell you the truth because I wanted to make sure you could handle it, and I wanted you to be ready to not only face your mom but face him too." Titus said.

"So that's what you meant all this time about God using me to tear down a corrupt religious system within a church? You were talking about our father's church the whole time?" Giovanni asked as Titus, Ramon and Preston nodded.

"Yes, that's right." Preston replied.

"See your mom went by Nikki back then. That's why we got it mixed up. Brianna, did you want to finish telling it?" Titus asked as Brianna nodded.

"Yes, please. Thank you. Baby, I know this is a lot but I can finish telling you what happened? These were the answers you wanted right?" Brianna replied as Giovanni nodded.

"I'll be right back, Gio. I'm going to go check on Chris." Asia said as she went down the hall to his room to check on Chris who had fallen asleep while on his ipad.

"So you found out you were pregnant when you took the test at Ceejai's house, got it. What happened after that?" Giovanni asked as Brianna paused for a moment before responding.

"The group had rules like of course making sure we told no one what we were doing for this money, we had to call our Pastor "*Daddy*" and the number one rule in the group was the no girl could get pregnant and if she did, she had to make sure she told Pastor in enough time to get an abortion. So that was the first thing Ceejai said to me when the test came back positive. She said we need to go find Daddy and tell him what happened so he can pay for the abortion." Brianna said.

"He was going to make you have an abortion so no one would know he was the father?" Giovanni asked.

"That and the fact that his wife had just found out she was pregnant with Ramon." Brianna said.

"So did you run away from Atlanta so that you wouldn't have to go through with the abortion?" Giovanni asked as Brianna cried more.

"Yes, I did. Pastor Hampton, my mom and Ceejai were pressuring me like crazy to do it. At first I said yes, but the day that I was supposed to tell Pastor Hampton that I was going to have the abortion, I got cold feet. I couldn't do it and I remember Ceejai getting made and freaking out on me because my mom and Pastor Hampton made it her responsibility to make sure I didn't change my mind about keeping the baby. So when I said I wasn't going to do it, she lost it! She told me if I didn't tell Pastor Hampton that I would have the abortion, I would end up just like the other girl named Brianna and I remember crying hysterically because they said it was an accident but we all knew otherwise. Brianna got pregnant by him too and she didn't want to have an abortion because she knew how money she would get a month in child support if she kept it and said that to him. They got into a fight and she was screaming at first, but then the screaming stopped. She died and they tried to say it was a suicide, but her family had been trying to get the police to re-do the autopsy for years but Pastor Hampton was a powerful man. I don't think anything ever happened after that." Brianna told him.

"So how did you end up in Miami?" Giovanni asked.

"When Ceejai said what would happen to me if I didn't go through with the abortion, I told her I was going to run away, have my baby and never tell anyone anything. I would just keep my baby safe and raise him or her to do way better than their mama. At that time, it was too soon for me to know if I was having a boy or a girl. I wanted a boy." Brianna replied.

"So your reasons for keeping me weren't like the other Brianna, right? I mean, you practically kept it a secret." Giovanni said.

"No, not at all. I didn't want anything from Pastor Hampton and I didn't care about the money I had been waiting all those years to get. I just wanted my baby so I packed up my stuff, got on a bus to Miami and never looked back. It was hard because I knew I was going to have to leave my sisters behind. But I was in danger if I stayed so I ran away. I tried to tell my sisters what was going on but Ceejai had already turned them against me. I don't know what she said but they didn't even want to talk to me so I left. I didn't have time to deal with them, you were the only person I could worry about protecting at that time." Brianna said as Giovanni nodded and Asia stood next to him again.

"So you came to Miami while you were still pregnant with me and that's when you met Derrick's mom, Sonja?" Giovanni asked.

"Yes, that's when I met her. We were staying right across the hall from each other and she was pregnant with Derrick the same time I was and she didn't have any support either so we became close." Brianna replied.

"So your Grandma and my aunts never tried looking for you? They didn't report you missing?" Giovanni asked.

"No, I'm pretty sure they moved on with life like I never existed. As far as I know, my mom and my sisters are still in Atlanta at Pastor Hampton's church but I don't know. We haven't seen each other or spoken since I left. Before today, I don't think anyone knew where I was." Brianna said.

"So Grandma and my aunts don't know you have four children?" Giovanni asked, still in shock as Brianna shook her head.

"They may know that I had one child but like I said, we haven't talked or seen each other since I was still pregnant so they didn't know I had a son and I know they didn't know anything about your sister or your brothers and I wanted it that way." Brianna said.

"So you never wanted to be found because you thought they would hurt you?" Giovanni asked.

"I knew the pastor would hurt me! If not him, he would get someone to do it for him. I had laid low all this time, that's why I never used social media and I didn't let you guys put pictures of me on your accounts. I needed to keep a low profile, but all of that was put in jeopardy today because of your sister!" Brianna said, sternly.

"Wait, before you tell me about that, I'm confused about a few things. Titus, if you, Ramon and Preston are my half-brothers, how have you been able to be here all this time spending time with me without getting your parents worked up about it? I mean, does your dad know about me?" Giovanni asked.

"No, he doesn't know about you. When your mom took off, he panicked at first and I won't lie, he was going to have someone track her down and kill her before she ever gave birth. But our mom talked him out of it. She's a nurse and she was convinced that because your mom would not have had the money or the resources to properly take care of herself under a doctor's care, she would have a miscarriage anyway. So he doesn't think your mom ever gave birth." Titus said.

"How did you find out about that if they didn't know?" Giovanni asked.

"We didn't know anything about you at first. By the time I was eighteen, I was through with my parents' and their twisted lifestyle and I wanted out. My dad wanted us to follow in his footsteps but I refused and so did Ramon and Preston. They were eleven and twelve when I got ready to graduate from high school and go off to college. I just so happened to get accepted into UF and I wanted to get away from my parents so I took it. Ramon and Preston were a little sad about it, but I still looked out for them and when their time came for college, they came to Florida too. What our dad didn't know was that I had made copies of his files to take with me so I could do my own investigation." Titus said.

"You took all of his files?" Giovanni asked.

"Not all of them, just the ones from the time that your mom was here. I wanted to start there because your mom was the only one that ever got pregnant by my dad." Titus said.

"How do you know that with so many girls?" Giovanni asked.

"I knew because your mom was the only one they ever talked about. Like I said, your mom went by Nikki because they already had another girl around her age named Brianna but I didn't find that out until way later. The entire time, I thought that maybe something happened to your mom after she left and that some girl named Nikki was the girl who got away carrying my dad's baby. I initially set out to see if I had another brother or sister out there somewhere." Titus said as Giovanni said.

"So when you met me, you didn't know you had it wrong until you met my mom at her apartment that day, right?" Giovanni asked.

"Well, yes. But I won't lie, we were suspicious when we met you and realized your last name was Ballard and we immediately started thinking about Veronica, Lauren, Kristen and Tia. But then I thought about Nikki. At that point I had yet to find her, not knowing her real name was Brianna Ballard." Titus said.

"My middle name is Nicole and everyone back then called me Nikki." Brianna replied.

"I thought we had it all wrong when you first told us your mom's name was Brianna. But then we saw her and even though it had been several years, I knew it was her. I knew that was Nikki and when I double checked the file again, it all made sense. But I had to use wisdom and I couldn't just come up to you and tell you everything that you're hearing now. At least not until the time was right. I knew God had connected the four of us for a reason and after you got saved, I was even more careful about the way I handled you and the things I told you." Titus said as Giovanni nodded.

"I get it. So you thought I was ready to hear it today?" Giovanni asked.

"Yes, I did. But I'm glad your mom was able to tell you first because she knew the parts I didn't know and plus I know you had been wanting your mom to open up for years." Titus replied.

"So Mama, what's with you and Asia fighting when I came inside? And Mama before you respond, promise me that from now on, you will keep your hands off of Asia. You've never hit me or any of my brothers the way you do her and after what you just shared with me, I think Asia is right. You despise her but it's not just because she's not a boy. She reminds you of how you were at her age. Right, Mama?" Giovanni said as tears fell from her face.

"Yeah, you're right. Fine, I won't hit her again and maybe if I get out of this alive, I'll apologize to her." Brianna said, sternly as Giovanni looked confused.

"What are you talking about?" he asked.

"The reason I grabbed your brother and came running out here to you was because late last night and early this morning, I could hear voices at one of my other neighbor's apartments. I saw Eddie, Jarvis and another guy I didn't recognize asking her if I stayed in the complex. Luckily she covered for me and said she didn't know me and it only gave me a few hours to gather as much stuff as I could into the car and drive away." Brianna said.

"My dad and Uncle Jarvis came looking for you?" Preston asked, surprised.

"He's your uncle?" Asia asked.

"Yes, that's our uncle. Jarvis is our mom's half-brother. By the way, Brianna, we think there's something else you should know." Preston asked as Brianna looked over at them wondering what he was about to say.

"What?" Brianna asked.

"It's been a while now but our parents got divorced." Preston said.

"Are you serious? So where's your mom now?" Brianna asked.

"She moved back home to Memphis and we told her that until she tells the police the truth and gets justice for all the victims she and our dad abused, she couldn't talk to us anymore. We haven't seen our mom since then. But it's okay because God is going to use Giovanni to speak up and speak out!" Titus said.

"That's right! When it happens, everything will be shaken up and there won't be anywhere left for our father, our mother, your mother or anyone else to hide!" Ramon said.

"I'm not speaking alone am I?" Giovanni asked as Titus, Ramon and Preston started laughing.

"Of course not, we will be right there with you! This is what we've been praying for and our moment is approaching!" Titus said.

"So your dad is single?" Brianna asked, still shocked at the fact that their parents divorced.

"No, he's not divorced anymore. He got remarried." Ramon said as Brianna looked surprised.

"He's remarried? Are you serious? Do I know her?" Brianna asked as Titus, Preston and Ramon glanced at each other.

"Yes Brianna, you know her. He married your mom. Her name is now Veronica Ballard-Hampton." Titus said as Brianna reacted to what they told her.

"What!? You're joking right?" she asked.

"No ma'am, we're not joking. They're married." Titus said.

"So wait a minute, you guys never told me about Jasmine." Giovanni said.

"Who is that?" Brianna asked, curiously as Giovanni pulled out his phone and showed her the picture on the school's athletic department website.

"Look Mama, her name is Jasmine Ballard. Nicholas came across her picture because she's an incoming freshman just like him on a basketball scholarship. We were wondering if she was related to us and then Nicholas ended up seeing Ramon and Preston talking to Jasmine at school." Giovanni said as Brianna continued looking at the picture.

"Yeah, I'm sure they know her. That's your cousin." Brianna said as she handed Giovanni back his phone.

"Really? That's my cousin? You guys knew that was my cousin?" Giovanni asked, glancing at Titus, Ramon and Preston.

"Yeah, we did. That's what we were talking to her about. We knew she would possibly cross paths with Nicholas and we told her not to tell him anything about her family if he asked her any questions." Ramon said.

"We figured Nicholas would be curious once he saw her last name was Ballard too. We didn't want anything leaking before we had a chance to talk to you ourselves." Preston told him.

"Wow, she looks just like Lauren. She's Lauren's daughter right guys?" Brianna asked as Titus, Ramon and Preston nodded.

"That's right, she's Lauren's oldest daughter. Lauren has two more daughters named Alicia and Natalie." Titus said as Brianna shook her head.

"She has two girls. I wonder if they had to go through what we went through." Brianna said.

"I doubt it. More than likely your mom didn't allow our dad to mess with them since they got married. But that doesn't mean there aren't other girls he's doing this to. He has a really big church." Titus replied.

"So Lauren is still in Atlanta at his church?" Brianna asked.

"Yeah, she's one of his ordained prophets." Preston said as Brianna shook her head.

"Yeah, I bet. So Kristen and Tia are there too?" Brianna asked.

"No, they're not there. I actually don't know where they are to be honest with you. We remember seeing them leave, but that was it. I don't think anyone has seen them since." Preston said.

"If you guys stopped going to your father's church and came to Florida, how do you know they left?" Brianna asked.

"They did some type of family honor day at the church and when your mom went up there with Lauren, Kristen and Tia weren't up there. They didn't even say their names, it was like they didn't exist." Titus replied as Brianna became concerned.

"So you don't have any idea where they might be?" Brianna asked.

"No ma'am, I'm sorry. We don't know." Ramon said as Brianna became concerned.

"I'm going to have to see what I can do to find them later but we have bigger problems on our hands.

"Eddie, Jarvis and that other guy came after me because of what Brianna did by showing Jarvis that picture. They probably think you know everything that went down, they may even be thinking that you're working with the police." Brianna said.

"Mama, I'm sorry. Are they going to come after me too?" Asia asked.

"Honestly Asia, I don't know. If anything, they will use you to get to me but I can't go back home until I get them off my back. Luckily Kyle doesn't come home for another few weeks so I'll only have to worry about Chris for now. I don't know what I'm going to do." Brianna said.

"I have an idea but we're going to have to move quickly!" Titus said as they gathered.

"I'm listening, Titus, what is it?" Brianna asked.

"Giovanni, I know your mom said it fast but you remember she said that the other Brianna who died had family who was trying to get the police to reopen her case and investigate it again to see if she was actually murdered?" TItus asked.

"Yeah, I remember..."

"Brianna had three brothers on her father's side who are triplets. While Brianna's mother took the money our dad paid her to keep quiet and ran off to West Palm Beach, Brianna's father and her brothers were trying to get justice. Brianna's mother had custody of her at the time that everything happened and I think Brianna's father always felt guilty for not protecting his daughter. One of Brianna's brothers is a police detective in Atlanta. I'm not sure if he was able to reopen his sister's case or not seeing as how no victims have attempted to come forward." Titus said, glancing over at Brianna.

"But he could reconsider opening up his investigation if we bring him something." Preston said.

"So we're going to Atlanta to see him?" Giovanni asked.

"Yeah, that's the plan. Are you in?" Ramon asked.

"Most definitely! This is what you've been preparing me for, right?" Giovanni asked as he slapped hands with Titus, Ramon and Preston.

"Yes and you're definitely ready!" Preston replied.

"Titus, why do you keep looking over here at me?" Brianna asked, nervously.

"I think you know why, Brianna. We need you to speak up. You don't have to confront our dad if you don't want to but if you could tell Brianna's brother the same story you just told all of us, it could reopen her case. Didn't you want justice for her after she died that night?" Titus asked as tears fell from Brianna's face.

"Yeah, I did. I always knew it wasn't an accident. Eddie silenced her for good so she wouldn't tell everyone she was having his baby." Brianna replied.

"Exactly, Brianna! Think about how much evidence and information was covered up to protect my father and to keep him from taking responsibility. The autopsy didn't even mention the fact that she was pregnant. I didn't recognize the name of the guy who did it but he was probably another one of my dad's minions that he easily paid to alter it." Titus said.

"I just don't see what good it would do for me to talk after all these years. I don't even have any proof that any of it ever happened. I mean, maybe if Ceejai or one of the other women who was in the group with me around the time came forward it would help. But I know they won't do it!" Brianna said as Titus glanced at Preston and Ramon. "Why did you look back at them? What?"

"I'm sorry Brianna, we thought you knew what happened to Ceejai." Titus said as Brianna's expression changed.

"No, what happened to Ceejai? I haven't seen or spoken to her since I ran away. She's okay right?" Brianna asked, concerned as Titus shook his head. "She's dead?"

"Yeah, she committed suicide six years ago. I looked her up online and read her obituary. I am so sorry, Brianna." Titus said as she started crying and shaking her head.

"I can't be too surprised. Ceejai went the hardest for Eddie and she probably got the money, went to school and everything didn't she?" Brianna asked as Titus nodded.

"Yeah, according to what I read she went to school at Florida State and graduated with honors." Titus said.

"She didn't have any kids did she?" Brianna asked.

"Yes, she left behind two daughters and a son. The website that had her obituary was located in Tampa so I'm assuming that's where her kids are living. Hopefully they're with family. The article didn't say much." Titus replied.

"What about Ebony, Janet, Marquitta and Brandy? Do you know where they are?" Brianna asked.

"Were those the other girls in the group with you, Mama?" Giovanni asked.

"Yeah, they were in the group with me and my sisters around that same time too. I mean Titus, you don't think any of them will come forward?" Brianna asked.

"No, they won't. They are still members at my dad's church today. None of them are married, they have children of their own and do you know what else they did?" Titus asked.

"What?" Brianna asked as Titus took a deep breath and sighed before responding.

"I don't really know how they made this happen but they legally changed their last names to Hampton." Titus said as Brianna and Giovanni reacted to what Titus said.

"What do you mean they legally changed their last names to Hampton? Why would they do that?" Giovanni asked, confused.

"To feel like they still belong to Eddie. Isn't that right, TItus?" Brianna asked.

"Yeah, unfortunately." Titus said.

"So wait, you said they had kids. They're not our dad's are they?" Giovanni asked.

"I'm honestly not sure. I don't want to believe your grandmother would be married to our father if he was having kids with women in the church, but this is the same woman who accepted money to keep quiet about our father sleeping with all four of her daughters, even after finding out that her oldest daughter was carrying his child." Titus said as Giovanni glanced at Brianna.

"Mama, you might be the only one who breaks this silence and tells this detective what you know." Giovanni said.

"Baby, I can't. I'm already on the run so they don't find me. You don't think they won't have eyes watching for me to go to the police? They will kill me and if they can't get to me, you think they won't figure out I have kids and come after one of you? I can't let that happen, Giovanni." Brianna said as she sat down and Giovanni pulled up a chair and sat in front of her.

"Mama, I get it. What if we promised that we would be able to keep you safe when we talk to the detective in Atlanta, will you do it?" Giovanni asked as Brianna shook her head.

"Even if I wanted to trust you on that, what proof do I have?" Brianna asked as everyone paused and thought for a moment.

"Do you have Giovanni's birth certificate?" Titus asked.

"Yeah, why?" she asked.

"His date of birth alone would be proof that you were still a minor when you had sex with Eddie if the detective does the math." Titus replied.

"Yeah, that's true. But do you think that and my testimony is enough to get them to reopen the case and get warrants to search his bank records and stuff like that?" Brianna asked.

"I can't promise you anything, Brianna. But I definitely think it's worth a shot. Will you come with us? We can do it this week!" Titus said.

"This week? Why so soon?" Brianna asked.

"I know it's a lot to do in a short window of time but my goal is the same night that Giovanni speaks up and exposes our father for the corrupt leader that he is, will also be the night that the police show up with warrants to arrest him and everyone that was involved!" Titus said.

"Even my mom?" Brianna asked.

"Yes, even her! I'm sure they will go after ours too even though she moved to Florida." Titus replied.

"So we're going to confront him in private or while church is going on?" Giovanni asked.

"It's going to be while service is going on and do you know what type of service that will be?" Titus asked.

"What?" Giovanni asked, confused.

"The Pastor's anniversary celebration!" Titus said as Brianna's facial expression changed.

"Oh my God, Titus! Is that coming up?" she asked.

"Yes ma'am, it starts next Friday night and it's going to last for seven days." Titus said.

"Next Friday?" Brianna asked, surprised.

"Yes, next Friday. That's why I want to get this ball moving so that we can expose him on the very anniversary that all of this started several years ago!" Titus said as Brianna nodded.

"Titus, you're right! I almost forgot that when these secret groups with the teenage girls at the church started, it was the week of his anniversary celebration which is usually always held around this time every year in the month of June!" Brianna said.

"Are you guys serious? We're coming up on the anniversary that all of this mess started?" Giovanni asked, surprised.

"Yes, we are and if we can get this ball rolling now, our plan could be executed that night. Even if the police didn't do anything, we're still going to speak out and the world is going to know the truth about Eddie Hampton! He invited a lot of people to this celebration so they're going to find out the truth about who they have been supporting all these years!" Titus said.

"Okay, I'll do it!" Brianna said as everyone got excited.

"Mama, you will?" Giovanni asked.

"Yes, I'll talk to the detective. Just don't make me go back to that church and promise you will help me find Kristen and Tia. I want to make sure they're okay even if they never talk to me again." Brianna said as Titus nodded.

"You have my word, Brianna. We will help you find them." Titus said as Brianna nodded.

"Thank you." Brianna replied.

"You're welcome." Titus said as they hugged each other.

"So when are we leaving?" Giovanni asked.

"Hopefully Thursday, no later than Friday. I need to call the detective and set up a time with him and make sure he's going to talk to us. When I tell him what I have, I think he will because he knows this involves his sister finally getting justice. So let me get that worked out and I'll get back with you. Is that okay?" Titus asked.

"Yeah Titus, that's fine. Thank you. Wow, I really can't believe you're my brothers." Giovanni said, smiling as they hugged each other.
"It doesn't change much does it? We've always considered you to be a brother to us!" Preston said.
"That's true. But you knew all along." Giovanni said as they laughed.
"You're not mad at us are you?" Ramon asked.
"No, not anymore. I understand and I appreciate you for wanting to take this stand. I know that it wasn't easy to go against your own parents." Giovanni said.
"It wasn't but we were tired of seeing this happen to girl after girl. The true church of God doesn't operate like this and it has been going on for too long." Preston said.
"Yes and we're about to see it all come to an end and everyone is going to get the justice they deserve. We want to see people set free and healed by the power of God, including you Brianna." Titus said.
"So is that the catch? I need to be converted like you did with my son?" Brianna asked.
"Not at all, Brianna. We're going with you all the way no matter what. But I wanted to make sure you knew that what we're praying and believing God for includes you and your children too." Titus replied as Brianna nodded and glanced at Asia who was

sitting on the sofa nearby drinking a soda and eating a bag of chips.

After about another ten minutes: Titus, Ramon and Preston left Giovanni's apartment and promised to follow up with him again tomorrow sometime once he had a chance to speak to the detective in Atlanta. Moments after they left, Chris came down the hall after waking up from his nap. Giovanni fixed him something to eat while Brianna and Asia started talking. Brianna apologized to Asia for all the pain she caused her. She apologized for rejecting her all these years and abusing her when she would hit her out of anger. It was exactly as Giovanni predicted. Asia was a reminder of who she once was and she hated the feeling of reliving her past by watching her daughter. It was why she prayed she would only have sons and not any daughters. Brianna asked Asia to forgive her and Asia said that she was still in a lot of pain and would work on getting to a place where she could fully trust Brianna and forgive her for everything she ever put her through. It was tough for Brianna to hear but she knew she had to accept it and allow Asia time to heal so they could hopefully have a better relationship one day as mother and daughter. Asia asked Brianna if she would be willing to tell them about their father too once Kyle got here and Brianna knew it would only be fair so she agreed to do it once he arrived.

Asia received a phone call from her two best friends that moved to Atlanta with her, Myeisha and Shonda who are cousins. They were really upset and

after Asia managed to calm them down, she asked
what was wrong and that was when they told her that
Jarvis fired them from working at the strip club as a
result of not being able to find her or Brianna. Asia
tried to explain to them what happened so they
wouldn't blame her for what happened but it was too
late and neither of them wanted to hear anything Asia
had to say. Before abruptly hanging up the phone,
Shonda and Myeisha told Asia they were no longer
friends and that they never wanted to see or talk to
her again because they were now going to have to
move back to Miami and live with their aunt who
never wanted them to leave in the first place. They
ended the call before Asia could say anything else.
Asia tried to call them back and they had already
blocked her number so she couldn't reach either one
of them. Asia started crying because she had been
friends with Myeisha and Shonda since elementary
school and she hated that they blamed her for what
happened. But she started to wonder if what they
said was right. None of this would have started had
she not shown Jarvis Brianna's picture and asked if he
knew her. Giovanni walked over and did his best to
console and encourage Asia not to blame herself as
she cried hysterically. It took a moment but Giovanni
managed to get Asia to relax and she nodded off to
sleep on the sofa. A couple of hours later, Nicholas
arrived at his apartment. Brianna and Giovanni took
turns telling him what happened while he was gone
and Nicholas couldn't believe his ears. He was even
more surprised to see that their mom had finally
opened up about her past and where she came from.

Brianna was now about to open up again by telling Nicholas and Asia the truth about their biological father. Since Kyle was at basketball camp, they used Skype to talk to him from Giovanni's laptop so Brianna could tell the three of them at once. They were shocked to learn that the four of them had the same father and what Brianna told them about having different fathers she knew nothing about wasn't fully true. Nicholas, Asia and Kyle have always had the same biological father. Brianna apologized for not telling them the truth all these years and explained that she had been too ashamed to admit to her children that she spent years in an abusive relationship with a man who became more like a pimp than her boyfriend. Brianna went on to explain that the only reason was able to get out of what she was in was because he died due to an accidental drug overdose. It was when she met Chris' father that she thought there would be a real future for their relationship because his dad accepted all of her children and treated them the same. But that was short lived when he was killed and Brianna never tried being with anyone again after that. Giovanni was happy that his mother was finally opening up to them and telling him and his siblings the truth about where they came from. But learning this truth made him more aware about the amount of pain and grief his family was in.

Giovanni's life really had not been the same since he gave his life to the Lord not long after meeting Titus, Preston and Ramon. Finding out that they were his half-brothers and that they had the same father who is a pastor in Atlanta was shocking and a lot to take in, but Giovanni knew that Titus, Preston and Ramon were right about the the fact that they always treated him like a brother and so much healing had taken place inside of Giovanni by their connection alone. Titus not only mentored Giovanni but he helped him take advantage of counseling which helped him address pain from his past that he was never able to talk about. Giovanni wanted the same healing and breakthrough for his family as well, especially after the transformation he witnessed with Chris overcoming his mental health challenges with school. Giovanni went to bed that night believing that what he was praying to see happen with his family would start with him being a voice for the voiceless.

By Friday, everything had been set up for them to travel to Atlanta. Titus spoke to Brianna Harris' brother, Jarrod Harris, II who is a police detective for the Atlanta Police Department. Titus was surprised and relieved when Jarrod explained to him during their conversation that he never stopped attempting to get justice for his sister. His supervisor had been allowing him to continue working his sister's death even though it was ruled as a suicide with the agreement that his pursuit would not interfere with his active cases. Jarrod was excited to hear someone finally say after so many years that they had a witness and victim from the time that Brianna Harris was alive who was ready to tell her story about what happened and provide information that would help Jarrod make an arrest and charge Pastor Hampton with multiple felonies. With school, games, practices and other events, Nicholas was not able to travel with them this weekend to Atlanta. But he was behind them all the way and he asked Giovanni to keep him up to date about everything as it happens.

Giovanni, Brianna, Asia, Chris, Titus, Dianna Ramon and Preston got off to an early start by leaving for Atlanta around five that morning so they could get there in enough time to settle in at one of the properties that he and his wife, Dianna owns in the area. No one was currently renting it out so they decided to stay there instead of paying for a hotel room. After arriving at the house and getting settled in, everyone went to lay down after they finished eating breakfast while Titus and Giovanni sat out back on the patio to talk more about their plans.

"Giovanni, I know you're tired after that long ride up here. Are you sure you don't want to get some rest before we go see Jarrod later on today?" Titus asked.

"I wasn't going to be able to rest until you told me everything else so we can talk first." Giovanni said as Titus nodded.

"Well I'll make it quick so we can both lay down for a while. We meet with Jarrod today at four o'clock at the police headquarters in downtown Atlanta." Titus said as Giovanni nodded.

"Do all of us have to go?" he asked.

"No, not all of us. Just you, me, and your mom have to be there. Everyone else can stay here at the house until we get back." Titus replied.

"Okay, that will work. So you said you, Preston and Ramon came up with an idea for how I would speak out at Eddie's church, right?" Giovanni said as Titus smiled a little.

"Yes we did and you're going to love it! When Jarrod told me how far along in his investigation for Brianna Harris he had already come, I knew this would work perfectly if I can get Jarrod to agree to it once he gets his warrants together from the judge." Titus said.

"Okay, I'm listening. Tell me!" Giovanni replied, anxiously.

"I'm friends with the guest speaker who is coming to speak on the first night of the pastor's anniversary. Her name is Capri Reynolds, we went to high school together and her dad is also a pastor here in Atlanta." Titus said.

"Wow, she's coming to speak for him knowing what he's done?" Giovanni asked, surprised.

"That's the thing, she didn't know before yesterday when I reached out to her." Titus replied as Giovanni reacted to what he said.

"What? But she was here in Atlanta too! There weren't rumors floating around about what was happening?" Giovanni asked.

"Not rumors from reliable sources. The couple of people who tried saying what they knew were former members and no one believed them. They assumed they were being bitter. Capri's dad used to preach for our dad often and he had no idea." Titus said.

"Wow, that's crazy. So why did you reach out to her after all this time?" Giovanni asked.

"I knew we were going to need her help getting your voice out in the open once and for all so I called her and I told her everything. She was in tears because she has a non-profit that supports young teens and women who have gone through sexual abuse and domestic violence." Titus said.

"She does? It's too bad she's not in Miami. She could probably help my mom and Asia." Giovanni said.

"There's a good chance she will be able to if they're open to it but I'll tell you more about that in a moment and she's going to explain it more when she comes by tomorrow." Titus said.

"Got it, so what's the plan?" Giovanni asked.

"Capri is going to come over here with her video equipment and we're going to have you do a video talking about everything. You're going to speak into the camera as if you're in the room with our dad talking directly to him! Once we save it, Capri's younger brother is going to play it when she gets up to speak. She's going to say that she has a video presentation for Pastor Hampton and that's when he will play it and he's going to do it in a way where no one in the church will be able to see that it's him playing the footage!" Titus said.

"Are you serious? That sounds amazing! How does he plan to do that?" Giovanni asked.

"The camera is going to be hooked into this special pair of glasses Capri's brother, Troy made. Troy is smart as what and a real nerd so the process

is long, but it's going to work! That's all that matters!"
Titus said.

"Man, I can't wait! This sounds good!" Giovanni
replied.
"The best part is that people everywhere will
see it because they're going to live stream the service
and I know a couple of reporters and journalists will
be there too. So this is going to blow up big! Once the
video stops, that's when Jarrod and his entire task
force will walk in with warrants to arrest our dad,
your grandmother and several other leaders in the
church who participated and helped him cover up
what he had been doing all these years!" Titus said as
he and Giovanni slapped hands.
"Wow, this is going to be amazing! Does my
mom know about this yet?" Giovanni asked.
"Not yet, you're the first one I told after
Preston, Dianna and Ramon of course! I'll tell
everyone else a little later. You're ready to do this?"
Titus asked as Giovanni nodded.
"Yes, I'm ready! Like you said, I've been
preparing for this moment!" Giovanni replied as Titus
nodded and gave Giovanni a hug. "I love you, man!"
"I love you too, Giovanni! I'm so proud of you!"
Titus said as Giovanni smiled and nodded.
"Alright bro, get some rest! We're getting
ready to shift things and this will be one pastor's
anniversary that our father will never forget!" Titus
said as he and Giovanni walked back inside the house.

THE PASTOR'S REVEAL

Tonight was the first night of the pastor's anniversary for Pastor Eddie Hampton where people locally and from around the world had come to spend the next seven days celebrating Pastor Hampton's fortieth year in ministry. What would typically be a night to honor integrity would soon turn into a night that would reveal the true heart, lifestyle and intentions of a corrupt pastor whose actions have killed one and caused severe trauma, pain and long term damage to many more including Giovanni's mother, Brianna Ballard. Giovanni arrived at the church with the rest of his family shortly after it got dark and they sat in the parking lot in Titus' black Suburban waiting for the right moment as they sat watching the service's live video from inside the truck. Jarrod and and several police officers were also in the parking lot sitting in unmarked police vehicles waiting for the moment that they would go inside the church and arrest Pastor Hampton with his other leaders while service was going on.

Giovanni went inside the church alone after receiving a text message from Capri's brother, Troy saying that he was ready for them to come inside. Nicholas wanted to go with him but Titus said it was best that Giovanni went alone so there wouldn't be too much attention drawn to the fact that Giovanni wasn't affiliated with any of the ministries represented at the service tonight. As Giovanni walked across the parking lot to the front entrance, Titus sent him a text message reminding him not to fill out anything with his name or information on it because their cover would be blown if anyone realized his last name was Ballard. Giovanni walked inside the crowded sanctuary and sat at the end of the third row next to Troy who was waiting for his queue from Capri to start the video. Capri was sitting in the pulpit as the master of ceremony read her bio and prepared to introduce her to everyone before she came up. Giovanni was blown away by the number of people that were inside the church to celebrate Pastor Hampton, many of them not having a clue about who he really is. But all of that was getting ready to change in the next few moments and Pastor Hampton's life and his church would never be the same again.

Moments later as Capri approached the podium and began to exhort and encourage the people who were standing on their feet clapping and cheering, Giovanni and Troy stood up as well so that they wouldn't look suspicious. Giovanni glanced at his phone and saw another text message from Titus that said that the police were going to make their move as soon as the video ended and he went on to explain that the entire building was now surrounded with officers who were prepared to take Pastor Hampton, Pastor Veronica Ballard-Hampton, and the others who were going to be arrested if any of them tried to leave. Jarvis Coleman and his three sons were arrested a half-hour ago and their strip club was shut down and everyone was sent home. Pastor Hampton's ex-wife, Felicia Coleman and Brianna Harris' mother, Katrina Nelson had been arrested by the local sheriff where they live and they were in the process of being transported to Atlanta. As everyone took their seats and Capri continued talking, she looked at Troy and gave him the signal to start the video which would project and play on the two flat screen televisions that were on the wall to the left and right side from where Capri was standing. The video started and about ten minutes in, everyone started to realize what was being said and they started to panic as Pastor Hampton stood and looked at the back of the church where his media team were sitting, signaling for them to turn the video off. One of the staff from the media room ran to the front of the church and told Pastor Hampton that they didn't start the video, they weren't sure where the footage was coming from.

When Pastor Hampton looked over at Capri, she had already grabbed her purse and ran out the side door before anyone could ask her what was going on. No one realized that Troy was sitting in the audience next to Giovanni controlling the footage that was being played loud and clear where everyone inside the church and online could see it. The reporters that were sitting at the back near the camera crew ran to the front to start questioning Pastor Hampton about the things that were being said about him and asking if he knew the young man that was in the video. Giovanni ended the video by revealing that Pastor Hampton started having sex with his mother when she was only 13-years-old, got her pregnant when she was 17-years-old and threatened to hurt her if she didn't have an abortion. Giovanni went on to explain that because Brianna managed to get away from him and her abusive mother who was now his wife, she didn't have an abortion but she gave birth to him. Giovanni ended the video by revealing to the world that he was the son of Edward "Eddie" Hampton who was getting ready to suffer the consequences for the murder of Brianna Harris and the years of sexual assault to his mother and several other young women. The video ended and the entire church went into an uproar as Pastor Hampton grabbed Veronica's hand and tried walking out of the side door and being met with several police officers who stormed into the church and arrested them both along with several of his leaders who were all sitting in the pulpit and on the front row.

The cameras caught everything and the local news station began reporting live what was happening from inside the sanctuary as people started leaving and running outside to see the arrest as Giovanni and Troy quickly grabbed their things and went out the side door on the other side of the church and stood outside with Capri who was waiting for Titus to pull the truck around without anyone seeing him. Titus quickly pulled up and Troy, Capri and Giovanni got inside as he drove down the opposite end of the street so that no one would see them.

As Titus drove down the street, Giovanni, Nicholas and everyone else started cheering because their plan worked and the arrests were finally made. Brianna sat next to Giovanni who had his arm around her, crying tears of joy as she watched her abusers on the local news finally get arrested because she knew that she, Brianna Harris, Cassandra "Ceejai" Johnson, and the many other victims who suffered in silence for all these years would finally get the justice they deserved. It was unfortunate that among those who were arrested, four of Eddie's former victims: Ebony Young, Janet Thompson, Marquitta Jones and Brandy Davis were arrested and charged for their being madams who helped Eddie and Veronica recruit girls for their private group and transporting them to dance at private parties for high paying clients who were pastors and leaders in other churches from around and outside of Atlanta. They were arrested for their involvement too.

This was something that many didn't think would ever happen, but the world would finally be able to see that it is possible to see that no matter how powerful and influential a pastor may seem to be, it is still possible to witness them be held accountable for their actions and not get away with illegal activity and behavior that ultimately impacts the lives of innocent people who in many situations are too broken to get themselves out of an abusive situation such as this.

Judgment would not only come for them in the justice system, but they would have to give an account to God for the blood that was now on their hands for scattering God's sheep, which were the men and women that they were commissioned to cover, pray for and handle with care. The exposure that was witnessed tonight was only the beginning of what's to come for Pastor Eddie Hampton and the other people that were involved. This was a night to remember and an anniversary that would never be celebrated again.

Jeremiah 23 (MSG)

"Doom to the shepherd-leaders who butcher and scatter my sheep!" God's Decree. "So here is what I, God, Israel's God, say to the shepherd-leaders who misled my people: 'You've scattered my sheep. You've driven them off. You haven't kept your eye on them. Well, let me tell you, I'm keeping my eye on *you*, keeping track of your criminal behavior. I'll take over and gather what's left of my sheep, gather them in from all the lands where I've driven them. I'll bring them back where they belong, and they'll recover and flourish. I'll set shepherd-leaders over them who will take good care of them. They won't live in fear or panic anymore. All the lost sheep rounded up!' God's Decree.

"Time's coming"—God's Decree—

"when I'll establish a truly righteous David-Branch,

A ruler who knows how to rule justly.

He'll make sure of justice and keep people united.

In his time Judah will be secure again

and Israel will live in safety.

This is the name they'll give him:

'God-Who-Puts-Everything-Right.'

"So watch for this. The time's coming"—God's Decree—"when no one will say, 'As sure as God lives, the God who brought the Israelites out of Egypt,' but, 'As sure as God lives, the God who brought the descendants of Israel back from the north country and from the other countries where he'd driven them, so that they can live on their own good earth.'"

The "Everything Will Turn Out Fine" Sermon

My head is reeling,

my limbs are limp,

I'm staggering like a drunk,

seeing double from too much wine—

And all because of God,

because of his holy words.

Now for what God says regarding the lying prophets:

"Can you believe it? A country teeming with
adulterers!

faithless, promiscuous idolater-adulterers!

They're a curse on the land.

The land's a wasteland.

Their unfaithfulness

is turning the country into a cesspool,

Prophets and priests devoted to desecration.

They have nothing to do with me as their
God.

My very own Temple, mind you—

mud-spattered with their crimes." God's
Decree.

"But they won't get by with it.

They'll find themselves on a slippery slope,

Careening into the darkness,

somersaulting into the pitch-black dark.

I'll make them pay for their crimes.

It will be the Year of Doom." God's Decree.

"Over in Samaria I saw prophets

acting like silly fools—shocking!

They preached using that no-god Baal for a
text,

messing with the minds of my people.

And the Jerusalem prophets are even worse—
horrible!—

sex-driven, living a lie,

Subsidizing a culture of wickedness,

and never giving it a second thought.

They're as bad as those wretches in old Sodom,

the degenerates of old Gomorrah."

So here's the Message to the prophets from God-
of-the-Angel-Armies:

"I'll cook them a supper of maggoty meat

with after-dinner drinks of strychnine.

The Jerusalem prophets are behind all this.

They're the cause of the godlessness
polluting this country."

A Message from God-of-the-Angel-Armies:

"Don't listen to the sermons of the prophets.

It's all hot air. Lies, lies, and more lies.

They make it all up.

Not a word they speak comes from me.

They preach their 'Everything Will Turn Out
Fine' sermon

to congregations with no taste for God,

Their 'Nothing Bad Will Ever Happen to You'
sermon

to people who are set in their own ways.

Have any of these prophets bothered to meet
with me, the true God?

bothered to take in what *I* have to say?

listened to and then *lived out* my Word?

Look out! God's hurricane will be let loose—

my hurricane blast,

Spinning the heads of the wicked like tops!

God's raging anger won't let up

Until I've made a clean sweep,

completing the job I began.

When the job's done,

you'll see that it's been well done.

Quit the "God Told Me This" Kind of Talk

"I never sent these prophets,

but they ran anyway.

I never spoke to them,

but they preached away.

If they'd have bothered to sit down and meet
with me,

they'd have preached my Message to my
people.

They'd have gotten them back on the right
track,

gotten them out of their evil ruts.

"Am I not a God near at hand"—God's Decree—

"and not a God far off?

Can anyone hide out in a corner

where I can't see him?"

God's Decree.

"Am I not present everywhere,

whether seen or unseen?"

God's Decree.

"I know what they're saying, all these prophets
who preach lies using me as their text, saying 'I
had this dream! I had this dream!' How long do I
have to put up with this? Do these prophets give
two cents about me as they preach their lies and
spew out their grandiose delusions? They swap
dreams with one another, feed on each other's
delusive dreams, trying to distract my people
from me just as their ancestors were distracted
by the no-god Baal.

"You prophets who do nothing but dream—

go ahead and tell your silly dreams.

But you prophets who have a message from
me—

tell it truly and faithfully.

What does straw have in common with wheat?

Nothing else is like God's Decree.

Isn't my Message like fire?" God's Decree.

"Isn't it like a sledgehammer busting a rock?

"I've had it with the 'prophets' who get all their
sermons secondhand from each other. Yes, I've
had it with them. They make up stuff and then
pretend it's a real sermon.

"Oh yes, I've had it with the prophets who preach
the lies they dream up, spreading them all over
the country, ruining the lives of my people with
their cheap and reckless lies.

"I never sent these prophets, never authorized a
single one of them. They do nothing for this
people—*nothing!*" God's Decree.

"And anyone, including prophets and priests,
who asks, 'What's God got to say about all this,
what's troubling him?' tell him, 'You, you're the

trouble, and I'm getting rid of you.'" God's Decree.

"And if anyone, including prophets and priests, goes around saying glibly 'God's Message! God's Message!' I'll punish him and his family.

"Instead of claiming to know what God says, ask questions of one another, such as 'How do we understand God in this?' But don't go around pretending to know it all, saying 'God told me this .□.□.□God told me that. .□.□.□' I don't want to hear it anymore. Only the person I authorize speaks for me. Otherwise, my Message gets twisted, the Message of the living God-of-the-Angel-Armies.

"You can ask the prophets, 'How did God answer you? What did he tell you?' But don't pretend that you know all the answers yourselves and talk like you know it all. I'm telling you: Quit the 'God told me this .□.□. God told me that .□.□.□' kind of talk.

"Are you paying attention? You'd better, because I'm about to take you in hand and throw you to the ground, you and this entire city that I gave to your ancestors. I've had it with the lot of you. You're never going to live this down. You're going down in history as a disgrace."

www.ingramcontent.com/pod-product-compliance
Lightning Source LLC
Chambersburg PA
CBHW072107150726
47999CB00005B/1938